Dear Parent:

Congratulations! Your child is taking
the first steps on an exciting journey.
The destination? Independent reading!

STEP INTO READING® will help your child get there. The program offers
five steps to reading success. Each step includes fun stories and colorful art.
There are also Step into Reading Sticker Books, Step into Reading Math
Readers, Step into Reading Phonics Readers, Step into Reading Write-In
Readers, and Step into Reading Phonics Boxed Sets—a complete literacy
program with something to interest every child.

Learning to Read, Step by Step!

Ready to Read   Preschool–Kindergarten
• big type and easy words • rhyme and rhythm • picture clues
For children who know the alphabet and are eager to
begin reading.

Reading with Help   Preschool–Grade 1
• basic vocabulary • short sentences • simple stories
For children who recognize familiar words and sound out
new words with help.

Reading on Your Own   Grades 1–3
• engaging characters • easy-to-follow plots • popular topics
For children who are ready to read on their own.

Reading Paragraphs   Grades 2–3
• challenging vocabulary • short paragraphs • exciting stories
For newly independent readers who read simple sentences
with confidence.

Ready for Chapters   Grades 2–4
• chapters • longer paragraphs • full-color art
For children who want to take the plunge into chapter books
but still like colorful pictures.

STEP INTO READING® is designed to give every child a successful
reading experience. The grade levels are only guides. Children can progress
through the steps at their own speed, developing confidence in their
reading, no matter what their grade.

Remember, a lifetime love of reading starts with a single step!

W9-ASG-592

For Christopher Pierce
—C.G. and D.G.

For the wonderful students and staff
at Loyola Village School, with love
—D.G.

Text copyright © 2010 by Charles Ghigna and Debra Ghigna
Illustrations copyright © 2010 by Diane Greenseid

Published in the United States by Random House Children's Books, a division of Random House, Inc., New York.

Step into Reading, Random House, and the Random House colophon are registered trademarks of Random House, Inc.

Visit us on the Web!
www.stepintoreading.com
www.randomhouse.com/kids

Educators and librarians, for a variety of teaching tools, visit us at
www.randomhouse.com/teachers

Library of Congress Cataloging-in-Publication Data
Ghigna, Charles.
Barn storm / by Charles Ghigna and Debra Ghigna ; illustrated by Diane Greenseid.
  p. cm. — (Step into reading. A step 2 book)
Summary: When a tornado touches down in a pond on Farmer Brown's property, it sets off a chain of events among the barnyard animals that soon has every creature displaced, but not unhappy.
ISBN 978-0-375-86114-7 (trade) — ISBN 978-0-375-96114-4 (lib. bdg.)
[1. Stories in rhyme. 2. Tornadoes—Fiction. 3. Domestic animals—Fiction. 4. Farm life—Fiction. 5. Humorous stories.] I. Ghigna, Debra. II. Greenseid, Diane, ill. III. Title.
PZ8.3.G345Bar 2010
[E]—dc22 2009033321

Printed in the United States of America
10 9 8 7 6 5 4 3 2 1

STEP INTO READING® STEP 2

Barn Storm

by Charles Ghigna and Debra Ghigna
illustrated by Diane Greenseid

Random House New York

A twister hit the pond
on Saturday night.

Catfish flew.

Frogs took flight.

5

Five frogs fell

in a barn full of hay.

They scared off the mule,
who ran away.

The mule crashed into
the chicken coop.
He chased all the chickens
in a loop-de-loop.

The chickens landed
in the old cornfield.

The cows all mooed.

The pigs all squealed.

The catfish fell
in the pigpen trough.

The catfish splashed.

The pigs took off.

The cows were scared
by the thunder's roar.

They ran to the house.
They knocked down
the door.

So that is why,
on Sunday morn,
there are frogs
in the barn
and chickens
in the corn.

There are fish
in the trough
and pigs in the pond.
The sun is shining
and the twister
is gone.

Old Farmer Brown
spent the night
underground

with his wife,

ten kids,

and their basset hound.

They yawned
and stretched,
then gasped
with alarm
at their mixed-up,
crazy, new
animal farm!

And that is why,
since Sunday morn,
the chickens are laying
eggs in the corn.

The frogs are jumping
in the loft full of hay,
and the mule is sleeping
in the coop all day.

The catfish are dancing

in a pigpen of mud.

A cow is in the kitchen
chewing on her cud.

The farmer's old house
is the cows' new home.

And the farmer's
ten kids never
have to sleep alone.

Life is very different
every morning
on the farm.
Now the mule hee-haws
the five o'clock alarm.

But the farmer
and his family
are growing mighty fond
of all the silly changes
since a twister
hit the pond.